This book belongs to:

_____

_____

_____

First US edition 2022

Library of Congress Catalog Card Number pending
ISBN 978-1-5362-2424-5

22 23 24 25 26 27 APS 10 9 8 7 6 5 4 3 2 1

Printed in Humen, Dongguan, China

This book was typeset in Lucy Cousins.
The illustrations were done in gouache.

Candlewick Press
99 Dover Street
Somerville, Massachusetts 02144

www.candlewick.com

Maisy Goes on a Nature Walk

Lucy Cousins

CANDLEWICK PRESS

Today, Maisy and her friends are going on a nature walk.

Maisy packs her bag.

Hooray—all ready to go!

Everybody meets at the park entrance.
"I'm so excited!" says Tallulah.

"Me too!" agrees Maisy.

First, they visit the pond.

There are so many animals
and plants living here!

Quack
Quack

Charley crouches down for a closer look.

Ribbit Ribbit

The animals who live in
the woods are very shy.
Who can you see?

Maisy spots a bird and her chicks.

Tweet
Tweet

Maisy looks for insects hiding under logs and in the leaves. The ants are very busy!

The next stop is the wildflower garden.
What's that buzzing sound?

The bees are busy making honey!

Buzz Buzz Buzz

Using a magnifying glass, Cyril looks at the tiny creatures living by the flowers.

Eddie finds the perfect tree to build a fort!

Maisy and Cyril collect little twigs.

Charley looks for branches and sticks.

Tallulah picks daisies for a special surprise.

What a marvelous fort!

"Surprise!" says Tallulah. She has made everyone lovely flower crowns.

"Thank you, Tallulah!"